The Wizard of Oz

retold by Carol Ottolenghi   illustrated by Jim Talbot

Copyright © 2002 Carson-Dellosa Publishing LLC. Published by Brighter Child®, an imprint of Carson-Dellosa Publishing LLC.
Send all inquiries to: Carson-Dellosa Publishing LLC, P.O. Box 35665, Greensboro, NC 27425.

Made in the USA.   ISBN 0-7696-6079-7   05-294137784

Long ago, a little girl named Dorothy lived on a farm in Kansas with her aunt, uncle, and dog, Toto. The family was poor, and life on the farm was tough.

"It's so gray here," Dorothy said one day. "I wish something exciting would happen."

"Well," said her uncle, "you might get your wish. A mighty big storm's coming."

Dorothy's aunt and uncle put her and Toto in the storm cellar for protection. Then, they ran to save the farm animals.

But Dorothy wanted to watch the storm. She snuck out of the storm cellar and crept back into the house. Suddenly, a tornado picked up the house with Dorothy in it! The house whirled and whirled. Then, it landed with a loud *thump*.

Dorothy peeked out of the door. "Toto," she said, "who are those people?"

"They are Munchkins," said a woman in white. "I am Glinda, a good witch. You landed your house on the Wicked Witch of the East. She ruled Munchkin Land very cruelly."

"I'm sorry!" said Dorothy. "I didn't mean to land my house on anyone. It was an accident. How do I get home to Kansas?"

"You will have to ask the Wizard of Oz," said Glinda. "He lives in the Emerald City at the end of the yellow brick road."

Glinda gave Dorothy the magical silver slippers from the Wicked Witch of the East. "These will protect you," Glinda said. "There are other witches in Oz. Not all of them are good."

The Munchkins showed Dorothy to the yellow brick road, and she and Toto set off to see the Wizard of Oz!

It was a long, hot walk. Dorothy and Toto stopped to rest. Dorothy looked up, and the scarecrow winked at her!

"Scarecrows don't wink," she said to Toto. "At least not in Kansas."

"Where is Kansas?" asked Scarecrow. "Are you going there now?"

"Soon, I hope," said Dorothy. "Wait a minute! Did you just say something?"

"Maybe," said Scarecrow. "I'm not sure."

"How can you not be sure?" asked Dorothy.

"I have no brain," said Scarecrow. "Just before the farmer put it in, the Wicked Witch of the West scared him, and he forgot."

"Come with me," said Dorothy. "The Wizard of Oz might give you a brain."

Dorothy and Scarecrow followed the yellow brick road. Toto ran ahead and discovered a man made out of tin! The tin man told them that he had been a real man, but the Wicked Witch of the West had changed him into metal. He did not have a heart anymore.

"Come with us," said Dorothy. "The Wizard of Oz might give you a heart."

They came to a dark forest. Suddenly, a giant lion leapt out and grabbed Toto. Dorothy whacked the lion on its nose.

"Ouch!" cried the lion. "I just wanted to scare him."

"Only bullies scare smaller animals," said Dorothy. "You are a coward!"

"I was not always a coward," said Lion, "but the Wicked Witch of the West stole my courage."

"If you behave yourself," said Dorothy, "you may come with us. The Wizard might help you, too."

They walked until they could see the Emerald City. The Wicked Witch of the West knew that Dorothy was helping Scarecrow, Tin Man, and Lion, and she didn't like it. So, she made Dorothy, Lion, and Toto fall fast asleep in a field.

Scarecrow and Tin Man called out for help, and Glinda heard them. She woke up Dorothy, Lion, and Toto, and they raced across the field to the Emerald City.

When they got there, the guard told them to go away.

"But Glinda the Good Witch told me to come see the Wizard," said Dorothy.

The guard gave them special glasses and then let them inside.

The special glasses made everything look green! "It's so beautiful," said Dorothy.

They walked through the streets until they reached the Wizard's palace. A guard stood at the door.

"Only Dorothy and Toto may see the Wizard of Oz," he said.

Slowly, Dorothy opened the door and tiptoed up the long hall. A giant head sat by itself at the top of the stairs.

"I never saw this in Kansas," Dorothy whispered to Toto.

"What do you want?" the Wizard asked in a low, rumbling voice.

Dorothy said that she wanted to go home. She told the Wizard about Scarecrow's brain, Tin Man's heart, and Lion's courage.

"I will help you all if you kill the Wicked Witch of the West!" said the Wizard.

The Wicked Witch of the West knew that Dorothy and her friends were coming for her. She ordered the flying monkeys to bring Dorothy and Toto to her castle. When they got there, the Witch flew into a rage!

"Those silver slippers protect you!" cried the Wicked Witch. "So, I can't hurt you or your little dog. But I can make you my servants. Scrub those stairs!"

The Witch hoped that Dorothy would take off the silver slippers while she cleaned, but Dorothy didn't. Suddenly, Dorothy slipped on the wet stairs. Her bucket of water spilled, splashing on the Witch.

"Ah!" shrieked the Wicked Witch. "I'm melting!"

Dorothy ran back to the Wizard of Oz. There, she discovered a secret. The Wizard was not a huge, scary head. The Wizard was really a man behind a curtain!

The Wizard helped Scarecrow, Tin Man, and Lion. He promised to take Dorothy home to Kansas in his hot-air balloon. But before Dorothy could climb into the balloon, a gust of wind swept it away, and she was stuck in Oz!

"Stay with us, Dorothy," said Scarecrow. "We love you, and it's beautiful here."

"I want to go home!" Dorothy wailed. "I miss my family! Glinda, can you hear me?"

"Yes," said Glinda. "Do you truly want to go home to Kansas?" she asked. Dorothy nodded.

"Then, close your eyes and click your heels together three times," Glinda said. "The silver slippers will take you home."

Dorothy closed her eyes. She clicked her heels together three times. Then, she opened her eyes and began to laugh.

"We're home, Toto," Dorothy cried. "We're home!"